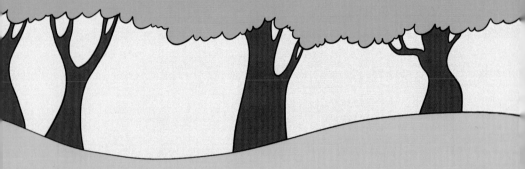

Published by Tate Publishing & Enterprises, LLC
127 E. Trade Center Terrace | Mustang, Oklahoma 73064 USA
1.888.361.9473 | www.tatepublishing.com

Tate Publishing is committed to excellence in the publishing industry. The company reflects the philosophy established by the founders, based on Psalm 68:11,
"The Lord gave the word and great was the company of those who published it."

Book design copyright © 2012 by Tate Publishing, LLC. All rights reserved.
Cover and interior design by Elizabeth M. Hawkins
Illustrations by Greg White

Published in the United States of America

ISBN: 978-1-61862-217-4
1. Juvenile Fiction / Action & Adventure / General
2. Juvenile Fiction / Imagination & Play
11.12.08

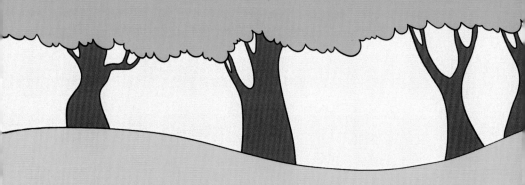

Dedicated to my family and friends.

On Monday they set out
on a ship to explore,
battling huge waves, rain,
and even lots more.

They ran into some pirates
and met Capt'n Kip,
who was tall and tough
and wanted their ship.

Tippi and Wilson were ready to fight.
But the pirates got scared
and flew out of sight.

All of a sudden they heard a noise
that was peculiar.
This noise was a voice
that was very familiar.

"Tippi, Wilson!
It's time to go!"

So, sadly, they left the ship behind
but knew they had more adventures in mind.

On Tuesday they traveled to the
rain forest to find a hidden treasure
that was once left behind.

Tippi and Wilson were very surprised with
what the treasure chest had hidden inside—
diamonds, rubies, and beautiful gold.
They knew these things
were important and old.

All of a sudden, they heard a noise
that was peculiar. This noise was a voice
that was very familiar.

"Tippi! Wilson!
It's time to go!"

So, sadly, they left the rain forest behind
but knew they had more adventures in mind.

On Wednesday they ran
through the scorching-hot desert,
searching for a hiding spot
from the lion named Chester.

They sank down behind
some very jumpy cacti,
and when the lion came upon them,
he started to cry...and this is why!

The jumpy cacti made a beard on his face. And
of course, this stopped the lion's chase.

All of a sudden, they heard a noise
that was peculiar.
This noise was a voice
that was very familiar.

"Tippi! Wilson!
It's time to go!"

So, sadly, they left the desert behind
but knew they had more adventures in mind.

On Thursday they traveled
to the jungle at night.
Treasure map in hand,
they stopped at a frightful sight!

Deep in the bushes
peered bright yellow eyes.
This creature had stripes
and seemed very wise.

All of a sudden, they heard a noise
that was peculiar.
This noise was a voice
that was very familiar.

"Tippi! Wilson! It's time to go!"

So, sadly, they left the jungle behind
but knew they had more adventures in mind.

On Friday they went to an
enchanted place full of wonder and mystery
and magical grace.

This place was a castle,
and there was a ball that night.
Everyone was dancing and filled with delight.

The ball was interrupted
when a dragon appeared.
The knights drew their swords,
and poof it disappeared.

All of a sudden, they heard a noise
that was peculiar.
This noise was a voice
that was very familiar.

"Tippi! Wilson! It's time to go!"

So, sadly, they left
the enchanted castle behind
but knew they had more adventures in mind.

On Saturday they discovered
a cave that was scary!
This place wasn't vacant,
but had bats that weren't very merry.

Stepping softly so they wouldn't be heard
traveling below.
But a bat was awoken,
and Wilson said, "Oh no!"

Tippi and Wilson ran, trying to get away
with the bats behind them,
flying their way.

All of a sudden, they heard a noise
that was peculiar.
This noise was a voice
that was very familiar.

"Tippi! Wilson! It's time to go!"

So, sadly, they left the cave behind but knew
they had more adventures in mind.

On Sunday they were swimming
in a lagoon,
suddenly noticing the strange shape
of the moon.

Tippi and Wilson felt something
bump their leg,
and to their surprise
appeared a beautiful mermaid named Meg.

They were fast friends
and started swimming and splashing.

They were all having fun,
playing and laughing.

All of a sudden, they heard a noise
that was peculiar.
This noise was a voice
that was very familiar.

"Tippi! Wilson! It's time to go!"

So, sadly, they left the lagoon behind but knew
they had more adventures in mind.

The week was over,
but the adventures were not.
A new week would begin,
which made Tippi and Wilson smile... a lot!

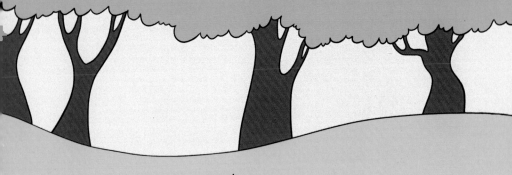

e|LIVE

---

listen|imagine|view|experience

AUDIO BOOK DOWNLOAD INCLUDED WITH THIS BOOK!

In your hands you hold a complete digital entertainment package. In addition to the paper version, you receive a free download of the audio version of this book. Simply use the code listed below when visiting our website. Once downloaded to your computer, you can listen to the book through your computer's speakers, burn it to an audio CD or save the file to your portable music device (such as Apple's popular iPod) and listen on the go!

How to get your free audio book digital download:

1. Visit www.tatepublishing.com and click on the e|LIVE logo on the home page.
2. Enter the following coupon code:
   d07c-3d11-fb7c-2cb6-a253-ae6b-44a2-e1c6
3. Download the audio book from your e|LIVE digital locker and begin enjoying your new digital entertainment package today!